P9-CDB-389

PURCHASED FROM
MULTNOMAH COUNTY LIBRARY
TITLE WAVE BOOKSTORE

Fun!

The Sound of Short U

By Peg Ballard and Cynthia Klingel

The Child's World®, Inc.

I can play in the sun.

I can have all kinds of fun.

I can play with my pup.

I can hold my body up.

I can play with a bug.

I can give a great
big hug.

I can feed a duck.

I can earn a buck.

I can run and run
and run.

I can have all kinds
of fun.

Word List

buck	pup
bug	run
duck	sun
fun	up
hug	

Note to Parents and Educators

The books in the Phonics series of the Wonder Books are based on current research which supports the idea that our brains are pattern detectors rather than rules appliers. This means children learn to read easier when they are taught the familiar spelling patterns found in English. As children encounter more complex words, they have greater success in figuring out these words by using the spelling patterns.

Throughout the 35 books, the texts provide the reader with the opportunity to practice and apply knowledge of the sounds in natural language. The 10 books on the long and short vowels introduce the sounds using familiar onsets and rimes, or spelling patterns, for reinforcement. For example, the word "cat" might be used to present the short "a" sound, with the letter "c" being the onset and "-at" being the rime. This approach provides practice and reinforcement of the short "a" sound, as there are many familiar words made with the "-at" rime.

The 21 consonants and the 4 blends ("ch," "sh," "th," and "wh") use many of these same rimes. The letter(s) before the vowel in a word are considered the onset. Changing the onset allows the consonant books in the series to maintain the practice and reinforcement of the rimes. The repeated use of a word or phrase reinforces the target sound.

The number on the spine of each book facilitates arranging the books in the order that children acquire each sound. The books can also be arranged into groups of long vowels, short vowels, consonants, and blends. All the books in each grouping have their numbers printed in the same color on the spine. The books can be grouped and regrouped easily and quickly, depending on the teacher's needs.

The stories and accompanying photographs in this series are based on time-honored concepts in children's literature: Well-written, engaging texts and colorful, high-quality photographs combine to produce books that children want to read again and again.

Dr. Peg Ballard
Minnesota State University, Mankato

Photo Credits

All photos © copyright: Dembinsky Photo Associates: 11 (Jean F. Stoick); Photo Edit: 8 (Tony Freeman), 12 (David Young-Wolff), 20 (Myrleen Ferguson); Photri: 16; Tony Stone Images: 3 (Bob Thomas), 4 (Andy Sacks), 7 (Bruce Ayres), 19 (David Hanover); Unicorn: 15 (Phyllis Kedl). Cover: Tony Stone Images/Myrleen Ferguson.

Photo Research: Alice Flanagan
Design and production: Herman Adler Design Group

Text copyright © 2000 by The Child's World®, Inc.
All rights reserved. No part of this book may be reproduced or utilized in any form or by any means without written permission from the publisher.
Printed in the United States of America.

Library of Congress Cataloging-in-Publication Data

Ballard, Peg.
    Fun! : the sound of "short u" / by Peg Ballard and Cynthia Klingel.
    p. cm. — (Wonder books)
    Summary: Simple text about playing and repetition of the letter "u" help readers learn how to use the "short u" sound.
    ISBN 1-56766-725-2 (lib. bdg. : alk paper)
    [1. Play Fiction. 2. Alphabet. 3. Stories in rhyme.] I. Klingel, Cynthia Fitterer. II. Title. III. Series: Wonder books (Chanhassen, Minn.)
    PZ8.3.B217Fu 1999
    [E]—dc21   99-31938
                                                              CIP